W9-BZL-362

The Berenstain Bears
and the
BAD HABIT

Habits & tics —

When cubs start to twitch
or to scratch or to nibble,
what they need is some help,
not a lecture or quibble.

Cub Care

A First Time Book®

The Berenstain Bears
and the
BAD HABIT

Stan & Jan Berenstain

Random House 🏠 New York

Copyright © 1986 by Berenstains, Inc. All rights reserved under International and Pan-American Copyright Conventions. Published in the United States by Random House, Inc., New York, and simultaneously in Canada by Random House of Canada Limited, Toronto. *Library of Congress Cataloging-in-Publication Data:* Berenstain, Stan. The Berenstain bears and the bad habit. (A First time book) SUMMARY: With the help of her family, Sister Bear breaks her habit of biting her nails. [1. Bears—Fiction. 2. Nail biting—Fiction] I. Berenstain, Jan. II. Title. III. Series: Berenstain, Stan. First time books. PZ7.B4483Beb 1986   [E]   86-3205   ISBN: 0-394-87340-8 (trade); 0-394-97340-2 (lib. bdg.)   Manufactured in the United States of America   4 5 6 7 8 9 0

Sister Bear, who lived with her mama, papa, and brother in the big tree house down a sunny dirt road deep in Bear Country, had been going to school for quite a while.

First there had been nursery school, which was pure fun—playing with dolls and blocks, rolling clay snakes, and scribbling with crayons.

Next had come kindergarten. That was fun too. There were marching games and rhythm band. She also learned a lot of numbers in kindergarten—and most of the alphabet.

1 1 1 1 1

2 2 2 2

3 3 3 3

4 4 44

Aa Aa

Bb Bb

Now Sister was in first grade. Regular school was different. It was still fun and she liked Teacher Jane very much, but it wasn't *all* fun. There was quite a lot of work—spelling, number problems, all kinds of things.

In regular school you have to concentrate—
and sometimes when you concentrate, you form
little nervous habits. That's what happened
to some of the cubs in Teacher Jane's class.

Lizzy twirled her fur.
Twirl, twirl, twirl.

Freddy scratched his head.
Scratch, scratch, scratch.

Norman sucked his thumb.
Suck, suck, suck.

And Sister nibbled her nails.
Nibble, nibble, nibble, nibble.

Before she knew it, she had nibbled them down to nubbins. In fact, she nibbled them down so far that some of her fingers were getting sore.

SCHOOL BUS

"Oh, dear!" said Mama Bear to Sister when the cubs got home from school one day. "You've nibbled your nails down to nubbins. In fact, you've nibbled them clean off. How did it happen?"

"I'm not exactly sure, Mama," Sister said. "But some of them are getting sore."

"Hmm," said Mama. "Well, here's what we'll do. We'll put a little medicine on the sore ones and bits of adhesive tape on all of them. That will remind you not to nibble and will give them a chance to grow back."

The bits of tape helped Sister remember not to nibble, but they also got in the way when she tried to do certain things. It's very hard to hold a pencil with tape all over your fingertips,

or tune the TV,

or scratch when you have an itch.

And when Sister tried to play jacks, she couldn't get any higher than twosies.

But worst of all, the
bits of tape told the
whole world that Sister Bear
was a nail biter.

The next morning, when Sister lined
up for school, Lizzy Bruin and
some others began pointing and
teasing. "Sister nibbles her nails!
Sister nibbles her nails!" It
didn't take Sister long to decide
to pull off those bits of tape!

And without the tape, she forgot
to remember not to nibble.

She forgot during school.

She forgot on the bus.

She even forgot as she
and Brother climbed off
the bus.

"You're going to have to cut that out, Sis," said Brother, "or you'll get to be a regular full-time nail biter."

"I'm afraid your brother's right," said Mama, who was organizing the wheelbarrow for some garden work. "I don't mean to nag, but nail biting is a very difficult habit to break."

"Habit?" asked Sister, making fists so that her nubby, nibbled-off nails wouldn't show. "What's a habit?"

"That's a good question," said Mama. "Come along while I plant these tulip bulbs Grizzly Gran sent over and we'll talk about it.

"A habit," Mama said as she pushed the wheelbarrow along the well-worn path, "is something you do so often you don't even have to think about it. Habits are a very important part of our lives. And most of them are good—like brushing your teeth and combing your fur when you get up in the morning, and looking both ways before you cross a road. But some habits aren't so good."

"Like nail biting?" asked Sister.

"You *would* like to have your nice nails grow back, wouldn't you?" was Mama's answer.

"Oh, yes!" said Sister. "But I keep forgetting! Why is it so hard to remember?"

"Well," said Mama, "it's sort of like this path. I've wheeled this barrow over it so many times that it's worn a deep rut right down the middle. And it keeps getting deeper every time I use it. Why, it's so deep now that I can't get out of it without a little help.

"That's the way it is with a bad habit—the more you use it, the harder it is to get out of it. Here, this is where I want to plant the bulbs."

"What about my nail-biting habit?" asked Sister as she helped Mama out of the deep rut. "How am I going to get out of it?"

"You just need a little help, that's all," said Mama. "Let's plant Gran's tulips while I think about it. And later I'll talk to your papa. He may have some ideas."

"I could read the riot act to her," suggested Papa. "You know: 'Nail biting is an outrageous, disgraceful habit and if you don't stop it immediately—'"

"Dear me, no!" said Mama. "Nail biting is a kind of nervous habit, and shouting and threatening will just make her more nervous."

"I suppose so," said Papa thoughtfully. "Perhaps some sort of reward would help. A bit of money—let's say a dime for every day she doesn't bite her nails."

Before Mama could answer, Sister Bear, who had been nervously nibbling in the next room, popped in and said, "A dime—ten whole cents every day just for not biting my nails?"

"That's right," said Papa. "Until the habit's broken."

"I'll never nibble again!" she said as she thought of all those lovely dimes she was going to get.

But the way it turned out, she didn't get a single dime. All she got was discouraged.

A day is a long time and habits are powerful—especially bad habits. Even with the promise of a dime, Sister couldn't remember not to nibble.

Mama and Papa got discouraged too.

"Oh, well," sighed Mama. "Life goes on. I must call Gran and thank her for the tulip bulbs."

"Oh, you're very welcome, my dear," said Gran when Mama called. "And how is everything at your house?...Is that so?... You know, I was a nail biter when I was a cub and my mama helped me to stop. What have you tried so far?...Um...Uh-huh... Well, I think you're on the right track with the dime, but instead of a dime, and instead of giving it to her at the *end* of the day..."

"What an interesting idea," said Mama as she listened to wise old Grizzly Gran.

So they tried Gran's idea. Instead of a dime at the *end* of each day, they gave Sister ten pennies—one for each nail—at the *beginning* of each day. Ten pennies to keep—*unless she nibbled.*

And with those pennies in her pocket,

jiggling when she got on the school bus,

jingling when she jumped rope in the schoolyard...

...just waiting to be remembered when some nail decided it needed a nibble...

the plan worked!

Not perfectly. It's hard to break a habit, and Sister had to give back some of those pennies. But in ten days she had ninety-three pennies!

But even better: she had
ten fine fingernails.

Great for picking things up,

tuning the TV,

and scratching itches.

And the next time she played jacks she got all the way to tensies!

"Phew!" said Papa Bear. "I'm glad that's over."

"Yes, indeed!" agreed Mama, breathing a great sigh of relief.

That's when Brother Bear looked at his fingernails and piped up, "You know, I think I might start biting my nails—I could use the money."

"I certainly hope you're joking!"
roared Papa. "Because if you're not—"
"I'm joking. I'm joking," interrupted
Brother.

And he was—sort of.